Dear Tree

To my parents, for giving me strong roots. D.R.W.

• • •

For my father and his woods of poplars and maples. P.S.

• • •

First Edition - January 2010 / Tevet 5770

PJ Library edition - November 2010 / Cheshvan 5771

Copyright © by HACHAI PUBLISHING

Artwork © copyright by Phyllis Saroff

Editor: D.L. Rosenfeld

Managing Editor: Yossi Leverton

Layout: Moshe Cohen

ISBN 978-1-929628-48-3 (Hardcover edition)

LCCN: 2009924430

HACHAI PUBLISHING

Brooklyn, New York

Tel: 718-633-0100 Fax: 718-633-0103

www.hachai.com info@hachai.com

Printed in U.S.A.

<u>Note:</u> In this book, the artist has drawn a variety of
the crabapple tree, one which has pink blossoms containing
five petals and tiny fruit less than two inches in diameter.

Dear Tree

A Tu B'Shvat Wish

by Doba Rivka Weber

illustrated by Phyllis Saroff

Hachai
PUBLISHING

Dear Tree,

May you have a year filled with sunlight...

...a year full of delicious rain.

May G-d give you...

...a year of chirping birds...

...and buzzing bees...

...a year of
beautiful blossoms...

...shiny green leaves,

and sweet fruit
with many seeds inside.

This year, I hope your bark
will protect your delicate branches.

I hope your branches will stretch out...

...and give more shade.

Stay strong, dear tree.
For a storm may rage,
and the sky may grow dark...

...but G-d has given you thick roots
that reach deep into the earth
to hold you steady against the wind.

May you stand, firm and straight,
for years to come...

...and may your seeds
grow into little trees
all around you.

So, dear tree,
I will care for you and guard you.

For I know that you,
and all other trees around the world,
do so much good for the earth...

...and for people just like me.
Happy New Year!